WITHDRAWN
S
Sullivan, Sarah
Root beer and banana /
WDWD 1066465137
WORN, SOILED, OBSOLETE

D0600656

For Kara, with everlasting gratitude,
and for Rick, who keeps on believing
S. S.

To Arnelle, Kendall, and Steven
G. S.

First edition 2005

Library of Congress Cataloging-in-Publication Data

Sullivan, Sarah.
Root beer and banana / Sarah Sullivan ; illustrated by Greg Shed. —1st ed.
p. cm.
Summary: Molly can't decide between two ice pop flavors one hot summer day, but the arrival of a new friend and some help from Granddaddy lead to the perfect solution.
ISBN 0-7636-1748-2
[1. Friendship—Fiction. 2. Sharing—Fiction.] I. Shed, Greg, ill. II. Title.
PZ7.S95355 Ro 2004
[Fic]—dc21 2002025990

2 4 6 8 10 9 7 5 3 1

Printed in China

This book was typeset in New Century Schoolbook.
The illustrations were done in gouache.

Candlewick Press
2067 Massachusetts Avenue
Cambridge, Massachusetts 02140

visit us at www.candlewick.com

ROOT BEER *and* BANANA

Sarah Sullivan

illustrated by **Greg Shed**

CANDLEWICK PRESS
CAMBRIDGE, MASSACHUSETTS

It's summer on the river,
when the air's as thick as soup
and you can smell tar
melting on the roof.
Sun's too hot for climbing trees
and we've already fished
our limit.

"C'mon, Squirt,"
Granddaddy says, giving me a wink.
"Time to stop by Mister Mac's."

TOLLIVER'S
FARM SUPPLY
GLENDA'S
ANTIQUES

Rolling over gravel
to the hard road, we drive
past Tolliver's Farm Supply
and Glenda's Antiques
to Mister Mac's General Store.

I can hardly wait
to get inside.

Mister Mac's ceiling fan stirs the heat
while the ice-cream freezer
hums its steady tune.

Cold air hits my face
when I slide the door open.
I stare at the colors
on the paper wrappers,
orange, cherry, and grape —
but the best flavors
are hidden underneath.

Banana or root beer?

Root beer or banana?

Which one will I choose?

I go outside to think it over,

leaving Granddaddy and Mister Mac

to swap stories—

who moved, who got married,

who has a baby coming—

the way old friends do.

Watching Main Street shimmer
under the noonday sun,
I see a girl waving
from the shade of
an old willow tree.

"What's your name?" she asks.

"Molly," I say.
"But my granddaddy
calls me Squirt."

She has bright yellow patches
on her dress with zigzag stitching
so they look like shiny suns.

"My name's Miracle," she says.
"On account of the doctor said
Mama couldn't have any more
after my brothers,
but I came anyway."

"I got some money," Miracle says.
"Wanna see?"
She opens up her palm
and shows me a nickel.
"I found it lying on the road," she says.
"I'm gonna buy something with it."

"What are you gonna buy?" I ask.

"One of those ice pops," Miracle says.

Ice pops cost a dime,
but I don't say anything.

"C'mon," Miracle says.
"I'll show you where they are."

She leads me to the freezer
and reaches inside.
"I want root beer," she says.
"Which one's that?"

I fish out the ice pop
with the brown wrapper
and hand it over.

"What's it going to be, Squirt?"
Granddaddy asks.
"Banana *and* root beer," I tell him.
He gives me a look.
I know what it means.

"Miracle needs one too," I explain.

"Miracle?" he asks.

"She's my new friend," I tell him.

"Pleased to meet you, little lady," he says.

Miracle pumps his hand.
"I live on Tucker's Creek," she says.
"Do you know where that is?"

"I sure do," he tells her.

“I’m gonna buy my ice pop
with this,” Miracle says.
“I found it lying on the road.”

“Well now,” Granddaddy says,
“which flavor’s for you?”

“Root beer,” she tells him.

“And banana for me, please,” I say.

Miracle holds out her nickel.

“That’s all right,”
Granddaddy tells her.
“This one’s on me.”

“Thanks, Mister,” Miracle says.
She tucks her money away.

I give Granddaddy’s hand
a big squeeze.

The screen door makes a lazy moan
when Miracle pushes it open.
Mister Mac's bird dog raises his head
to see if we have anything
for him, but we tell him
ice pops aren't for dogs.

"Would you like to trade halves?" I ask her.
"You can have half of my banana,
and I'll have half of your root beer."

"That's a good idea," she says.
"That way we get a taste of both."

So I help her break her ice pop
and she helps me with mine.
And we sit together
under the shade of
the old willow tree,
eating root beer and banana,
banana and root beer,
and swapping stories,
the way old friends do.